Al.   ... ... per Lin

www.HarperLin.com

New Year's Slay

❄

An Emma Wild Mystery

Book #2

by Harper Lin

ISBN-13: 978-0993949548

ISBN-10: 0993949541

Contents

Recipes

Chapter 1

If I hadn't known any better, I would've thought that Martha Owens got staked through the heart by a vampire slayer. That was the first thought that came into my mind when I saw her limp body on the ground in the Sweet Dreams Inn. But it wasn't a wooden stake through her heart; it was simply the largest knitting needle I had ever seen. It stuck right out from her chest while blood stained the lower part of the needle, along with a good portion of her lavender cardigan set.

"Oh my god," I gasped.

A police officer stepped in front of me before I could get any closer to the body.

"Ma'am, you're not allowed to be here."

Before I could protest, Detective Sterling Matthews stepped forward and waved him away.

"It's okay, Peter, she's with me."

Sterling smiled and winked at me. He raised his arms for a hug, but his arms went right back to his sides when he saw that I wasn't making my move to greet him the usual way—with a big hug and a kiss on the lips.

"What a way to ring in the new year, huh?" Sterling said.

"Who would do this?" I asked.

"I was just asking your friend the same thing."

I looked up at Nick Doyle – the movie star and my ex – standing in a corner of the living room. Eyes wide and hugging himself, he was clearly shaken.

Sterling had been questioning Nick before I showed up, which was why Nick called me right after he called his lawyer. Nick was the only guest at the inn, and the only person who saw Martha last before her death. And he was the prime suspect.

I didn't know Martha Owens too well, but I knew of her because she owned the only inn in Hartfield. The only other lodging for visitors was a seedy motel a half hour's drive away. Martha was also in my mom's knitting group, but from the way my mom talked about the dynamics of the group, it didn't sound like she was very well liked. Even Mom, who generally got along with everybody, hardly ever invited Martha over.

Funny enough, I did speak to Martha three days before she was murdered when I went to the inn to talk to Nick.

When he showed up in Hartfield on Christmas Eve, he caught me kissing Detective Sterling Matthews in front of my house. Nick and I had broken up a few weeks before and I had moved out of the New York penthouse apartment that we shared. After holing up in a hotel for a week, I decided to come home to Hartfield to spend time with my family for the holidays.

I didn't expect to reconnect with Sterling, who was my high school sweetheart and my first love that I never completely got over, but I did and I was happy, until Nick arrived with the most beautiful diamond engagement ring I had ever seen.

I thought that Nick would go back to New York and never speak to me again after finding out that I had moved on with Sterling, but he surprised me by staying. Nick was angry at first, but he took a couple of days to cool off. He wasn't the type to stay angry for long, and he knew that I wasn't to blame because we had already broken up and I was under the assumption that he had already moved on with a Victoria's Secret model thanks to the tabloids. However, it turned out that the rumors weren't true.

I never expected Nick to come here and propose. For a while, I believed what the press said about him – that he was heading to a lifetime of bachelorhood à la Leonardo Dicaprio. I was pushing thirty and Nick hadn't proposed after four years of living together, so I gathered my pride and my designer clothes in a suitcase and left him. But now it turned out that he did want to marry me. Practically every girl wanted to marry Nick Doyle. But I couldn't just drop Sterling; I had feelings for him too.

As one of the biggest movie stars in the world, Nick was used to getting what he wanted. I guess when I left he realized what he had taken for granted. I had to be careful with him. Who knew if Nick really meant it? Sterling and I were starting to have a good thing going. I'd never stopped loving him. But I never stopped loving Nick either. The decision to be with Sterling had been easy when I believed that Nick didn't love me enough. Now, I was beyond confused.

Nick called me a few days after Christmas and told me that he was still in town.

"I thought you'd be back in New York by now," I said.

"You can't get rid of me that easily. I waited a while to call you to get my head straight."

"Are you mad?" I asked.

"I was, but I want to talk to you in person. Can we meet?"

I was hesitant. While we weren't official, I was back with Sterling, but I knew that I owed Nick a face-to-face chat if he had come all the way to Hartfield with an engagement ring.

"Sure. Where are you staying?"

"The Sweet Dreams Inn."

I stifled a laugh. Somehow I couldn't quite picture Nick staying in Martha's quaint little B&B when he was used to five-star accommodations. With her floral wallpaper, ornamental plates on walls, pink bed sheets and an excess of pillows and cushions, Sweat Dreams was a grandmother's dream.

"There are no other hotels in sight," he explained. "Where else could I stay?"

"True," I said. "Should we meet there then?"

"Yes. There's no one else staying here at the moment."

"Did anyone recognize you?" I asked.

"Martha has no clue. I only told her that I was in town alone nursing a broken heart so that she'd feel sorry for me."

"You didn't." I laughed.

"Now she wants to set me up with the daughters of a few of her friends."

"Hmmm."

"Since you're taken, I might take her up on that offer."

"If that's what makes you happy," I said.

"Glad to have your blessing," Nick joked.

At least Nick was back to his jovial self. He was like a cat, always landing on all fours whenever he was thrown. If I stayed with Sterling, Nick would be all right. The question was, would I?

We made plans to meet at the inn for afternoon tea.

Sweet Dreams was on the outskirts of town, near the lake. It was run by Martha Owens. Ever since Martha's divorce ten years ago, she'd been running the inn alone. Her husband had moved to Vancouver and got remarried.

Tourism had dwindled in recent years. But Martha had too much of a sentimental attachment to the inn to ever sell it. She had grown up there, and her son had grown up there as well. Maybe Martha was fine living in what was really an empty Victorian mansion.

The upside to the lack of business was that Mom's knitting circle was welcome two times a week in the inn's lounge, a.k.a. the living room. The group had nineteen members and the inn was one of the few places in town that could host such a large group of chatty senior ladies armed with sharp needles.

I passed by Samford Street, where the massive Christmas tree and all the decor and lights on the lampposts and shops were still up. Boxing Week was still going strong. The locals went into stores in droves and came out with more shopping bags than they had before Christmas. My sister's cafe was as busy as ever, and I waved to her outside the window when I passed by, but she didn't see me. I was relieved that the murder last month in her cafe hadn't affected sales, but the whole incident was another story – something I was trying to push from memory going into the new year.

When I reached Sweet Dreams, Nick was standing on the porch waiting for me.

His dirty blond hair was neatly parted and combed, reminding me of that rockabilly character he played in one of his movies. He was tall and fit, especially coming off filming the sequel to his action film Alive or Dead. His hands were shoved deep into the pockets of his black wool jacket and he was shivering.

Even though he was thirty-three, he reminded me of a boy who needed to be taken care of, and I supposed he brought the maternal instinct out in most women, which was part of the reason why he was such a hit with them. I wanted to scold him for not wearing a scarf in December weather, yet wrap my arms around him to warm him up.

When he saw me, his blue eyes lit up and he cracked his dimpled smile that made me – and every other girl in the world – melt. I smiled back, but I really wanted to sigh in frustration. Why did he have to be so good looking?

He came down and hugged me. "I missed you."

"Let's go inside," I said. "You look like you're freezing."

"Is it always this cold in Canada?"

"You have to ask? Winter barely just started here."

The inn was beautiful, but in that creepy Victorian way. As a child, I used to be afraid of it because rumor had it that it was haunted. The outside was painted a dark teal with even darker window shutters. The interior was like the inside of a dollhouse. Everything was perfect and antique. Martha was in her rocking chair, knitting away. Time stopped inside that place.

When Martha saw me, she got up and greeted me.

"Beth's daughter," she said. "I haven't seen you for a while. Heard you ran off to the city and became a singer."

Martha was nearly sixty. Her curly short hair was dyed an orangey blond color and she wore bifocals that enlarged her brown eyes. I didn't know what to make of her. She'd scared me as a child because she always seemed cranky and I was told not to get on her bad side because she had a temper. Kids always knew to stay away from her place on Halloween if they didn't want day-old fruit and a lecture about candy causing cavities.

"I did," I replied.

"I always saw you singing around town and now I hear you're singing in New York?"

"That's right."

"I hope that you're making a living. Are they paying you well?"

Nick and I both tried not to laugh. Martha didn't seem to have a clue that I had two best-selling albums and a Grammy award for best album of the year.

"Yes," I said. "They are."

"Good." She smiled. "Your mom said you were doing well." Martha turned to Nick. "See, young man? I told you that there are plenty of pretty young women for you in this town. You'll get over that nasty ex-girlfriend in no time."

I raised an eyebrow. "Oh?"

Nick chuckled nervously. "She wasn't all that bad, Martha..."

"She sounds awful," Martha said vehemently. "Who could break this handsome young man's heart and jump into the arms of another young man? A floozy, that's who."

"She sounds horrible," I said, not sure whether to laugh or get mad.

"You deserve better," Martha said to Nick.

"Er, thanks." Nick rubbed the back of his neck. "We'd like to have some tea, please."

"Oh, sure," said Martha. "I didn't mean to intrude on your date. Of course. Sit yourself in the library and I'll bring you some tea and desserts. I just made fresh blueberry scones this morning. Do you like those?"

"Yes," we said in unison.

"Then I'll put on the kettle and bring you everything when it's ready."

The library was a nook around the corner from the living room. Two walls were lined with books, mainly mystery novels and a very heavy encyclopedia set. There were three sets of tables and chairs, all empty, and we sat at one table.

"I'm sorry about that," Nick apologized.

"So you've been talking about how awful I am, huh?"

"I was mad when I first saw you and that guy kissing, so I vented a bit, but –"

"It's fine," I said quickly. "I get it. It's a complicated situation and I didn't mean to hurt you."

"You know why I'm back," Nick began. "I didn't know that you would move out so suddenly. I mean, I really didn't see it coming."

"That was one of the problems," I said slowly.

"I know, I know." He sighed. "It's difficult for me to have a relationship, with all the traveling that I do. I always have a million things going on."

"Yes, well, I didn't want to get in the way."

Nick leaned forward on the table and took my hands. "You weren't. I was the idiot. I realize that I took you for granted."

His hands felt warm over my cold hands. How did he manage to warm them up so fast when he'd been freezing outside only moments earlier? I didn't move my hands away, but I didn't say anything either.

"I realize now that when you were talking about marriage and everything, you meant it. I was so stupid. I didn't think you were serious because we were living together and we were happy. Or *I* thought we were happy. Heck, I thought I *was* committed because you were the first girl and only girl I'd ever lived with. Aside from my mom."

I laughed. Nick never failed to make me smile even in serious situations.

"You have to admit that all things considered, living together was rather a big step for me."

"But we'd been living together for four years,"
I said. "For some girls, that may be enough, but
I'm a traditional, small town girl. I want to get
married and have kids. But aside from that, it just
didn't seem as if I was a priority in your life. All the
filming, the promotional tours, the charity events –
I understand that they're all important to you, but
for a while, we were roommates who hardly saw
each other. I was the one flying out to you most of
the time."

"Which is why I'm here," he said. "I'm ready to
make a commitment. Come on, Emma. Please give
me another chance. I love you."

His last words seemed to echo in the little
library. I had to take into consideration that he was
an actor, and that he could say a line pretty well.
But I also knew him well: Nick wasn't the type to lie.

"What about those lingerie models?" I asked.

"The thing with models is that they are, well,
for a lack of a better word, easy. They're pretty and
they're fun, and I dated them when I was younger
when I wasn't looking for something complicated.
But now I'm ready. I want to be in a meaningful
relationship with a complicated girl. The ring is still
for you. What do you say?"

If Sterling weren't in the picture, I would've said
yes. But I was hung up on Sterling. Most of my

songs on my first album were about him. You never forgot your first love.

When it rained, it poured. Just weeks ago, I thought I was better off single because I couldn't find a guy to commit, but now Sterling also wanted to be in a serious relationship with me. He said so on our last date.

"You know that I'm dating someone else," I said finally.

Nick sighed. "But whoever that guy is, he's a rebound and you know it."

I shook my head. "He's actually an ex-boyfriend. We've known each other since high school."

"High school sweethearts, huh?" Nick's smile fell and there was a harsher note in his voice. "Are you spending New Year's Eve together?"

I nodded. "I'm sorry, Nick."

On New Year's Eve, my family was throwing a party with close friends, and Sterling was coming over. I couldn't invite Nick too.

He looked crestfallen, but he kept his hands over mine.

"Then I'll be here," he said. "I'll wait right here at this inn until you're ready."

"Why would you assume I'll be ready?"

"Because you haven't said no."

He was right. I hadn't said no. He still had a chance, and he knew it.

"Like I said, Emma. I'm going to fight for you this time. I don't care who this guy is, and how long you've known each other. You love me and I love you. It's as simple as that."

I wasn't so sure about that. I never knew love to be so simple, and that belief was evident in my songs.

Chapter 2

The Wild house was pumping with cheesy eighties music. Dad was dancing to Cyndi Lauper's "Girls Just Wanna Have Fun" and trying to get Mom to join in. We'd invited fifteen guests comprised of close friends and family. My very pregnant sister, Mirabelle, was here with her husband, and our childhood friends Suzy and Leslie and their boyfriends. Most of the other guests were invited by my parents. Sylvia and Rhonda, Mom's closest friends from her knitting group were over as well.

I was relieved that Martha wasn't here. Because Sterling was invited, I didn't want her slipping in the fact that I had been on a "date" with Nick at her inn. Things with Sterling were still new and I wasn't exactly sure what to do. For now, I did want to give Sterling another chance. There was a lot of catching up we needed to do.

He showed up clean-shaven and smelling like the ocean. He offered me a bowl of mashed potatoes, sheepishly admitting that he'd made it with his daughters earlier that afternoon.

"This looks great," I said.

He beamed and quickly kissed me before anybody behind me noticed he was here.

"Sterling," my mom said. "Glad you could make it.

My parents knew by now that I had broken up with Nick. I didn't tell them – Dad had stumbled onto an article about our breakup when he was on the *Huffington Post* website – and they had a good idea that I was still sweet on Sterling.

Mom took his coat and winked at me when she thought Sterling wasn't looking. I stifled a groan.

While there was more than enough food and drink for our guests, everybody brought a dish of their own and the party turned into a potluck. After I introduced Sterling to the other guests, I put his mashed potatoes on the kitchen counter already crammed with other bowls and plates of an assortment of dishes, appetizers and desserts.

"Help yourself if you're hungry." I pointed to the self-serve plates and utensils.

"Don't mind if I do." Sterling grinned at the selection and began loading up his plate.

"That's too bad your girls couldn't come," I said.

"They're with their mom," he said, "at their grandparents' house. But they're with me next weekend. Would you like to come over and meet them on Saturday?"

"Sure!" I said. "I'd love to."

I thought it was sweet that Sterling was so close with his daughters and I did want to meet them. He had divorced a couple of years ago, but seemed to have a civil and practical relationship with his ex-wife. I never knew his wife because he'd met her in college, and in a way I was curious about her.

I didn't mind that Sterling was divorced. It was so commonplace to have starter marriages now, especially when people married young. I thought it was great that Sterling became a dad. I'd always thought that he would make a great dad.

Maybe I was getting too ahead of myself, but I considered the possibility of becoming a stepmom. Would his daughters like me? Or would they resent me? What if I wasn't good with kids?

I told myself to relax. So far I'd only been on two official dates with Sterling.

Suzy and Leslie's boyfriends came by the table and began to chat Sterling up. There was a shortage of men at the party, so they stuck together. They talked about hockey, beer and whatever else it was that men bonded over.

I quit listening to the boys and wandered over to Mom and her knitting friends. When Mom got pulled into another conversation by one of Dad's golf friends, Sylvia and Rhonda teased me about my date.

"He's certainly a handsome fellow," said Sylvia.

At seventy, she was the oldest member of mom's knitting group. With her white hair, friendly face and cheerful demeanor, she reminded me of Betty White.

"If only I were forty years younger," Rhonda said. She was tall, big-boned and had shoulder-length gray hair.

Sterling was certainly handsome of the tall, dark variety. He had stormy gray eyes that made him look like he was constantly brooding. How different he was from Nick, Hollywood's golden boy. While Nick was outgoing and charming, Sterling was quiet and thoughtful. Nick was a popular celebrity, while Sterling stayed in the shadows to dig up the cold hard truth for his line of work.

Trying to choose between them was like picking between apples and oranges, but both had enough hold on me to break my heart. What they had in common was that they both did at one point. I'd written enough songs about those heartbreaks. But it was almost the new year. I would start fresh and leave the past pain behind. The question was—who would I choose to spend my future with?

Sylvia giggled. "He looks just like this boyfriend I had when I was in my twenties and living in Rome for the summer. Is he Italian?"

"I don't think so," I said.

I was so amused that they were giggling over Sterling like schoolgirls that I got pulled into it too. For a while, I gushed about what Sterling did and how great he was. Then I asked them about how their knitting group was going.

The knitting gang met every Tuesday and Thursday at Martha's inn and Sylvia wasn't happy about the location.

"I keep telling the group that we should change venues," she said. "I don't like that inn of hers."

"Why not?" I asked.

"It's haunted," she said matter-of-factly.

"Oh, don't mind her," Rhonda said. "Sylvia thinks a lot of places are haunted."

"It's true," Sylvia protested. "This town was built on an Indian burial ground."

"Have you seen a ghost?" I asked. While I didn't know if I believed in ghosts, I was intrigued by the whole thing.

Sylvia nodded. "When I went in to the bathroom once at Martha's, I was washing my hands and saw a white figure reflected in the medicine cabinet mirror, but when I turned around, there was no one there."

"Maybe because there was no one," Rhonda said. "It could've been your overly active imagination."

"I saw it," Sylvia insisted. "You couldn't pay me to sleep in that house. No wonder the place hardly ever has guests. I would rather stay on someone's couch than that creepy place. I just get a really bad feeling every time I go there."

"Who do you think is haunting the place?" I asked.

"I don't know," said Sylvia. "But whoever is there is bringing a very heavy energy."

"We began holding meetings there when I couldn't host at my daughter's house anymore," said Rhonda. "My daughter had kids and the house became too chaotic for so many old ladies. Plus, I thought that since Martha had so much space, we would open the group up to new members, but it didn't turn out that way."

"I voted to let in new members too," Sylvia exclaimed. "Knitting has become popular with the younger women in town and some of them had expressed interest in joining. I thought it would be nice to have some young blood in the group, but Martha simply refuses."

"It's like she's in charge now!" Rhonda huffed. "Just because she's hosting doesn't mean she calls the shots. Sylvia and I are the founding members. It's completely unfair, so at the next meeting, we're going to insist on having a vote about this matter. And if Martha doesn't like it, well, we'll just have to find a new venue."

I nodded sympathetically. "I wonder if Mirabelle's cafe can be a potential venue. It's just so busy most of the time, but otherwise, I'm sure she would love to host you."

"We'll see, dear," Sylvia said, smiling. "It's just that there are so many of us that most establishments don't allow it. Your mom offered your home, which is very nice of her. We might take her up on it. We would fill the whole living room, but if worse comes to worse, at least we have a backup plan."

"I hope our house is not haunted," I joked.

"It's not," Sylvia said with a serious expression. "If it was, I would tell you."

"We used to meet in the town library," Rhonda said. "But that place is too quiet for a bunch of noisy old ladies like us. Plus the librarians disapprove of us because of our knitting needles. They say it's dangerous around the kids."

"Imagine calling us dangerous," Sylvia said, chuckling. "But I guess they have a point. It could be dangerous if a child took one of our needles from our bags without any of us noticing and ran around with it."

"Well, I hope things work out," I said.

"It would be great to include new members and pass down our techniques," Sylvia said.

"Knitting secrets." Rhonda winked. I laughed.

"It's just a matter of the members voting and agreeing on some things," Sylvia. "It's so silly. All the knitting politics."

Rhonda looked at her wristwatch. "My, it's getting late."

"But it's only ten forty-five," Sylvia said.

"I'm sorry, ladies. I promised my daughter I'd go home to count down to the new year with the family."

Rhonda said farewell to us and the rest of the guests while Sylvia and I continued to chat.

"I sure hope to get out of that inn." Sylvia shuddered. "It gives me the creeps. Have you noticed that crows always like to stand on the roof over there? That's never a good sign."

Aside from her ability to see ghosts, Sylvia surprised me by announcing that she could also read palms. She told me that I would have a long full life. I'd marry and have up to four children if I wanted to.

"Would it be soon?" I asked.

"It's up to you," said Sylvia. "You still have free will of course. This is just a guideline of what's in store for you. Lines do change however."

"Really? Lines can change on a palm?"

"Why, certainly."

I looked over at Sterling, wondering if he was the guy I'd end up with. He already had two children. If we married, I'd only have to give birth twice to have the big family that I wanted. That was, if his first wife didn't mind me spoiling her daughters.

But I also wondered how Nick was getting on. Was he still in Hartfield? If he was, he would be spending New Year's Eve alone. I knew it was silly, but I also worried about whether the inn really was haunted. When I was there last, I did sense a certain Victorian creepiness about the place, but I was there in the daytime. I was sure that it was much spookier at night.

I checked my phone. Nick did call. I listened to my voicemail. Nick left a message, wishing me a happy new year. He didn't say where he was. Wherever he was, he sounded lonely.

When the countdown began, everyone was so drunk and happy. Sterling pulled me in close and gave me a slow, sensual kiss when we reached midnight. I would've been lost in that kiss if I wasn't aware that my parents were hovering around us somewhere in the living room.

Was he a better kisser than Nick? I didn't know. They were just...different.

But I couldn't help but think about Nick and what a great time we had last New Year's Eve in Aruba, partying it up at a hotel party with a group of our friends. Nick was fun, which wasn't to say that Sterling wasn't, but I wondered about our lifestyle compatibility. Sterling was rooted in Hartfield, while I needed to travel and tour the world for weeks or months at a time. Either way, I had a busy lifestyle to work around.

I decided that my New Year's resolution would be to not worry so much. For now, I tried to enjoy the moment.

But I kept itching to call Nick back because of how sad he sounded. I restrained myself.

On New Year's Day however, Nick called me, but his news was more bizarre than anything I expected to hear.

Chapter 3

"I didn't kill her," Nick said.

It was ten o'clock in the morning on New Year's Day. There was panic in Nick's voice. I didn't blame him when I heard what had happened.

When he went downstairs for breakfast in the morning, he stumbled onto Martha's dead body and stepped into her pool of blood.

"Of course you didn't kill her," I exclaimed. "I totally believe you."

"Can you please come down and tell that to your boyfriend?"

Oh no. Sterling was there already. I jumped out of bed and pulled out some clothes from my closet.

"I'll be there as fast as I can," I said.

After gargling down some mouthwash, dressing and twisting my red hair into a messy bun, I ran down the stairs, grabbed my coat and started running to the inn.

I saw Martha's body with that big knitting needle still stuck in her chest as soon as I ran through the door. A photographer was snapping away at the body as if this were one of my magazine cover shoots. Sterling stepped away from interrogating Nick to tell the policemen blocking my path that it was okay that I was there.

"This is unbelievable," I said.

Nick looked pale. He had dark circles under his eyes and his hair wasn't neatly combed and gelled as it usually was. He came over and hugged me.

"Are you okay?" I asked Nick.

"Fine." He tried to look brave, but it was obvious that the scene made him queasy. I took him into the library, while Sterling hovered nearby.

"What happened?" I asked Nick. "Start from the beginning."

He sighed. "Yesterday night, I ate dinner with Martha. I didn't really feel like celebrating the new year. Martha was kind of glum too because her son had plans and hadn't spent New Year's Eve with her. So we both decided just to retire early. I went up to my room and dozed off. Never heard a thing. Then I found her like this in the morning..."

I nodded, knowing that when Nick was asleep, it took a lot to wake him. It was why he usually set three alarm clocks when he needed to wake up for early shoots or important events.

"Poor thing," I said. Nick's eyes were rimmed with red and he was rocking from heel to toe as he spoke as a way of soothing himself.

"Your boyfriend seems to think I had something to do with it," he continued.

"I just want to get all the facts," Sterling said. "You were the last person to see Martha and the first person to find her dead. It seems a bit odd that you didn't hear anything. There was a sign of struggle. Martha could've been screaming for help. You're telling me that you didn't hear her scream or hear any voices at all?"

"Like I told you," Nick said through gritted teeth, "I'm a deep sleeper. Plus my room is at the end of the hall. It wouldn't have been loud enough to wake me."

"It's true," I told Sterling. "Nick doesn't wake up very easily. I can attest to that."

"There's no sign of a break-in," Sterling said. "Nick's fingerprints are everywhere and I wouldn't be surprised if they were on those needles as well."

"I'm a guest here!" Nick exclaimed. "Of course my fingerprints are going to be everywhere. If they weren't, I'd be a ghost. But I can assure you that they are not on those needles. I've never even seen those needles before. She usually knits with normal needles."

"We'll see about that," Sterling said. "Didn't you have some anger issues on the set of a film a few years ago? Where you reprimanded a crew worker and there was a recording of you swearing and having some sort of nervous breakdown? Maybe that temper of yours got the best of you. Maybe Martha didn't make your chicken dinner the way you liked it and you got peeved."

Nick's face grew red. "Not that this is any business of yours, but there was a reason I was angry at that crew member."

I knew the story. The crew member in question had been secretly filming Nick on set and selling gossip about him to the tabloids. The guy ultimately got fired, but unfortunately, his video of Nick freaking out over his invasion of privacy still leaked and went viral.

"I'm not some spoiled actor. Martha and I got along great. Emma can attest to that. She was here a few days ago."

Sterling looked at me in surprise.

"I was here," I admitted. "Nick wanted to talk so I came over for tea. He was indeed very friendly with Martha and she seemed to like him. There's no reason why Nick would want to hurt her."

Sterling grew silent, his gray eyes brewing a storm. I could feel him tensing up.

"Even so, the circumstances surrounding Nick are questionable." Sterling turned to Nick. "As much as I hate to say this, you have to stay in town until we find out more."

With that, Sterling turned back to the scene of the crime to rejoin his team. Nick rubbed his face with his hands.

"It's okay, Nick," I said. "We both know you're not guilty."

"This is a disaster," he said. "How can she be murdered?"

"Is the door locked at night?" I asked. "Or did Martha keep the door open for any last minute guests?"

"She locked it," he said. "At least she usually did. She had a curfew. At ten o'clock she would lock the doors, so if I ever needed to go out, I had to tell her so she could give me a key to let myself in late at night. I remember her giving me a lecture about not staying up late or doing anything 'sinful.'"

"And what time did you go to bed?"

"Around nine thirty."

"Did you sleep right away?"

"No. I was probably up until 10:30 p.m. watching TV before I dozed off."

I smiled, imagining Nick falling asleep in front of the TV. It was a common habit of his and I usually had to turn the TV off and put a blanket over him.

"This means that she must've let the killer in," I said. "It was probably someone she knew."

"She didn't seem to be too well liked," he said. "She constantly complained that she wasn't invited to any New Year's Eve parties."

I recalled what Sylvia and Rhonda had said about her and how my mom hadn't invited her to the party because she was too much of a downer.

"It does sound like she butt heads with others a lot," I said.

"She could be very judgmental," Nick said. "And I think she had a lot of bitterness built up, but ultimately I think that she was a vulnerable person. As far as I was concerned, she was nice to me."

"And to me too," I said, recalling how attentive Martha was when I was over for tea.

"She's just someone who's used to getting her way and hates it when others ignore her."

I was touched by how much sympathy Nick had for Martha. He always treated older women well. He was very close to his mother.

"Well, it looks like you don't have a place to stay now," I said.

"That's right."

"You're welcome to stay with me," I offered.

"Sure," he said softly. "That would be great."

Nick smiled at me in gratitude. I smiled back. He was close enough to kiss me, but I stood up from the table. I took a peek out at the crime scene. The photographer had left, but a new man had entered the house.

He wore chunky black-rimmed glasses and, when his back was turned to me, I noticed that he was starting to go bald. His face twisted into an expression of pain as he looked down at Martha's body. Sterling reassured him and took him aside.

"Who would do this?" he cried. "Who would ever want to kill my mom?"

The man began to sob into his hands.

"I can't be here," he said. "I can't look at her."

Nick came up beside me.

"Shoot," Nick said. "It's Cal, Martha's son. Poor guy."

Sterling took Cal outside.

I turned back to Nick.

"Get your stuff so we can go to my house."

While Nick went upstairs to pack, I looked around the place. The forensic team was all over the living room, so I sneaked into the kitchen and looked around. All the dishes had been done. The glasses on the drying rack were all spotless. Martha must've been a clean freak. I checked the garbage can. It was empty except for a white knitted scarf. I could tell it was homemade and it had cable stitching. Maybe Martha threw it out because she was dissatisfied with the results, although I saw nothing wrong with the scarf.

Nothing else seemed to be out of place and I was disappointed that I had nothing more to go on.

Nick came downstairs with his leather duffel bag, ready to go. There was little else to do except to find out more about Martha Owens.

Chapter 4

We passed Sterling and Cal in deep conversation on the porch on our way out. They didn't notice us so I didn't say goodbye. I felt sorry for the guy. Imagine seeing your own mother's murdered body.

"They shouldn't have let him see her body like that," Nick said. "That's not right. It's traumatizing."

"I can imagine." I had also seen another dead body recently and it wasn't exactly pleasant.

We walked for a good ten minutes back to my house, passing the charming, snow-blanketed town. It was bittersweet walking with Nick through Hartfield. I'd often pictured us doing this but didn't think we'd do so broken up and leaving a murder scene.

"I heard that the inn is haunted," I said as we walked past the shopping area.

"Haunted?" Nick raised an eyebrow. "Really?"

"So you didn't notice anything weird? No strange noises, shadows, or anybody pulling off your bed sheets in the middle of the night?"

"No. Do you believe in that?"

I shrugged. "Not really, but it's fun to think about."

"I guess being in that big house knowing that the other rooms are empty can be kind of creepy. I didn't exactly want to hang out in the hallway alone in the middle of the night. Why? Have there been ghost sightings?"

"This lady from my mom's knitting group claims to be sensitive to spirits and that she saw something once in the bathroom."

"Ohh, a toilet phantom."

I cracked a smile. "Don't worry. There are no ghosts at my place. Just a couple of elves living in the attic."

Both of my parents had met Nick on many occasions and seemed to like him, but this was the first time that Nick ever visited me in Hartfield.

When Mom answered the door, she was shocked to see him. She knew that we had broken up and she wasn't aware that he'd been in town all this time.

She quickly covered her surprise with a warm smile.

"It's a lovely home you have, Mrs. Wild."

My dad came in from the kitchen. "Nick?"

He looked confused as well. They both knew that I was dating Sterling now.

I explained that Nick was here to visit – although I didn't say that he'd brought a diamond ring along – and told them what had happened to Martha the night before.

"Oh dear," Mom exclaimed. "Poor Martha."

She sat down and looked pale. Dad went to get her a glass of water.

"Nick has to stay here for a while," I said. "He's a witness. I hope that's okay."

"Of course it is," Mom said. "Who would do this to Martha?"

"We don't know yet," I said.

Mom stared into space and looked to be in deep thought about who Martha's killer could be. I wanted to grill her about what she knew, but thought it was best to let her think for a bit.

I led Nick up to the second floor and showed him the guest bedroom, the one next to mine. The room used to be Mirabelle's, who now lived with her husband in a house in the same neighbourhood. Even though Nick and I had lived together for years, having him in such close proximity made me nervous. What if the temptation to be together was still there?

"I'm sorry you had to get mixed up in all of this," I said.

"Who knew small towns could be so dangerous? In all my years of living in New York, I had never seen a dead body or knew of anyone who was murdered. The irony."

"Why don't you lie down and have a rest for a bit? I'll go down and see about lunch. I'll come and get you when it's ready."

"Thanks, Emma." Nick smiled.

I couldn't help but feel responsible. If it weren't for me, Nick wouldn't have had to stay in that inn. Taking care of him was the least I could do.

Downstairs, Dad made his famous chili, while Mom was still on the couch, digesting the news.

"This is horrifying," she said to me. "To think that this could happen in Hartfield. I wish there was something that I could do."

"I'm sorry, Mom." I hugged her. "Maybe we can do something, by figuring out who would hurt her."

"That would be difficult because Martha didn't get along with a lot of people. Even I didn't particularly see eye to eye with Martha most of the time. She could just be so negative and overbearing that it drove you nuts. But even so, she meant well, and she could be generous under that rough exterior. She didn't deserve this."

"Of course not, Mom. I'm sure we'll catch the killer. Sterling's investigating right now."

She looked up at me. "What is Nick doing here? I thought you two had broken up."

I slowly explained that Nick had been here since Christmas, and that he wanted to get back together.

"Why, that's wonderful. Although, Sterling..."

"I know, I know. I'm trying not to think about it right now."

She patted me on the knee. "Don't worry, honey. You'll know who the right one is when it's time."

"Thanks. Right now I just want to help catch this guy."

"If I tried counting all of Martha's enemies on my fingers, I wouldn't have enough hands."

"Was there anyone that Martha particularly hated?"

"Well, I only know Martha through the knitting group. Otherwise, we're not close enough to spend quality time together."

"Did she butt heads with a lot of the women in the group?"

Mom thought about it. "Yes. She had plenty of disagreements with Rhonda and Sylvia, because they are the founding members of the group, and Martha was starting to boss the group around more and more, but I've known Rhonda and Sylvia for years. They wouldn't kill her."

I didn't comment on that. Sometimes the person you least suspected could surprise you the most. Instead, I told Mom that Martha was stabbed with a gigantic knitting needle.

"Just how big was the needle?" Mom asked.

"They were the thickest I'd ever seen. As thick as my wrist."

Mom's eyes grew wide. "Martha didn't own those needles. They're Rhonda's."

"What? Really?"

"Yes. You can't find those needles in Hartfield. Rhonda had to order them from an online knitting store and it took quite a while for them to be shipped here."

"Maybe Martha ordered them too."

Mom shook her head. "I don't think so. Rhonda had them during the last meeting, and she was showing them off quite a bit. Martha really wanted them. If Martha ordered them that day, the needles wouldn't have gotten here so fast, especially with delivery being so slow around the holidays."

"What about express shipping?"

"She would never pay for express shipping. Martha was, well, cheap about those kinds of things."

I stood up and paced. "Do you think that Rhonda could hate her enough to kill her?

"Rhonda's one of my closest friends!" Mom exclaimed.

"I know, Mom, but sometimes people do regrettable things when they're angry. I'm not saying Rhonda did it; I just want all the facts to piece this together. Can you tell me more about what they argued about?"

Mom slowly nodded and considered her words carefully. "Rhonda and Martha have had their disagreements, but they usually tried to be civil about it. Sylvia and Martha butt heads a lot, and Rhonda usually comes to Sylvia's defense, so Martha tends to feel a bit outnumbered sometimes. But Martha can be bullheaded and downright aggressive when she argues. She can be a bully to many members of the group."

"Sylvia was at our party on New Year's Eve," I said.

Mom nodded. "And your father drove her home."

"Rhonda left early. She said she was going home, but she could've stopped by Martha's easily."

"To think that Rhonda could murder someone..."

Mom still couldn't wrap her head around this possibility, but the evidence was starting to point Rhonda's way. I recalled the scene this morning at the inn. A new ball of lavender yarn had rolled loose on the floor, and a bunch of regular needles poked out from a bag. A yellow scarf was in the process of being completed with a pair of these normal-sized needles and it rested on top of the bag. It meant that Martha was already working on something. Maybe Rhonda came in, there was a scuffle and she stabbed Martha at the height of her anger.

Dad poked his head in from the kitchen door. "Lunch is ready. Emma, do you want to call Nick down?"

"Sure, Dad."

I ran back up and knocked on Nick's door. He had fallen asleep and groggily sat up when I came in.

"Nick, did you ever see Martha knit?"

"Yes, all the time."

"Did you ever see her knit with those big needles?"

He thought about it. "I recall Martha talking about knitting. She said she was finishing a scarf to donate to sick children at the hospital. Those were with regular needles, I think. That was yesterday. I don't know if she was knitting with those big needles or not."

"But you would notice if she were knitting with big needles, right?"

"Maybe," said Nick.

He wasn't the most reliable guy when it came to details. Sometimes he'd go days without noticing that I had gotten my hair cut.

The only way to find out whether those needles were Rhonda's was to go to the source.

Chapter 5

I knew that Rhonda was in her late fifties. She lived with her daughter's family and owned a cheese shop on the corner of Samford Street and Marble Avenue.

I didn't want to tell Sterling about the needles belonging to Rhonda just yet. I was afraid that he'd be too tough on her and frighten her with his questions when all I wanted for now were some simple answers. If Rhonda was the killer and she was comfortable speaking to me, she might let something slip.

Another reason I didn't want to talk to Sterling was that I wasn't ready to talk to him yet. I was sure he was mad at me for seeing Nick, and he would be more upset to know that Nick was staying with me now too. I knew I had to talk to him sometime, but not before I gathered the info that I wanted to support my case.

Many of the shops on the main shopping streets were open on New Year's Day, including Mirabelle's Chocoholic Cafe. Rhonda's cheese shop, *Cheese,*

Please, was also open. I was glad because I had an excuse to see Rhonda.

I picked up a few things from the supermarket to make it seem as if I was just shopping before I entered *Cheese, Please.*

"Hi, girls," I said brightly.

Sylvia and Rhonda were both behind the counter wearing red gingham aprons. They were all smiles at the sight of me.

"Hello, dear! Have you tried our cheese of the week?" Sylvia pointed to the cheese samples on the counter.

"Mmm, Gouda." I didn't even like cheese that much but tried one anyway.

"Food shopping, already?" asked Rhonda. "Thought you had plenty after last night's bash."

"Actually, most of the food is gone," I said. "Everyone kept eating well into the morning."

"Sounds like some party," said Rhonda. "I guess things really began to heat up after I left."

"Are you looking for anything in particular?" Sylvia asked.

"I'll take this," I said about the Gouda. "Dad loves cheese. I'm sure he'll like this one."

"It's from The Netherlands," said Sylvia.

"Do you know that they have a little cheese museum in Amsterdam?" said Rhonda. "I would love to visit sometime."

Guessing by their cheerful demeanors, they hadn't heard about Martha's death. Or perhaps Rhonda was simply feigning ignorance.

"Have you heard about Martha?" I said.

"What about Martha?" Sylvia asked.

I told them that a guest at her inn found her murdered this morning.

Shock splashed across both of their faces. Sylvia gasped.

"Oh my God," said Rhonda. "How?"

"She was stabbed with a knitting needle. A very chunky needle the size of my wrist."

Rhonda turned white. "Oh, Jesus."

Sylvia turned to Rhonda with her mouth open and I held my breath, anticipating Rhonda's admission. How would she get out of this?

"Those are my needles," Rhonda admitted.

"Your needles?" Sylvia said. "How can you be sure?"

"Because I let Martha borrow them."

"When?" I asked.

"Last night," Rhonda said, her voice shaking. "I had agreed to let her borrow them, but I'd forgotten to give them to her yesterday. When I opened my trunk to store my empty Tupperware from your party, I saw the needles there, and I decided I'd just go and give them to Martha, since her inn was on the way home."

Sylvia frowned. "But you just got those needles. Why would you let her borrow them?"

Rhonda hung her head a bit. "Well, I didn't want to tell you, but Martha wanted to kick you out of the knitting group."

"What?" Sylvia exclaimed.

"She was trying to convince the other members that you were...crazy. Martha was very offended that you kept calling her house haunted and creepy, and wanted to vote you out of the group."

"But..." Sylvia looked hurt. "How could she?"

"You know how vindictive she can get when she feels wronged. I was trying to talk her out of it, to not start any drama that would cause more arguments in the group. That was the only way the group could survive. As a peace offering, I lent her the needles, knowing how much she liked them. She planned on making a shawl with them. That was the deal. She got the needles until hers came in the mail, and she'd drop this little war on Sylvia. I think what she really wanted was control, because she was so lonely. Her son moved out and she had nobody to listen to her anymore, except us. I knew she didn't have anywhere to go on New Year's Eve. She wasn't invited anywhere. It was late, but her light was on, so I went to see her. I thought she would welcome the company, so I chatted with her a bit about her knitting project. She was cranky when she answered the door, but she was in a better mood when I left, probably because someone actually came to visit her. Although she'd be too proud to admit any of this."

"Was anyone else in the inn?" I asked.

"Not that I was aware of. I heard no voices. Although..." Rhonda paused, something obviously striking her. "When I was driving away, I did see a pickup truck pull up in front of the inn."

"Did you see who it was?" I asked.

"No. It was too dark, and I didn't think much of it."

"What color was it?"

"I don't know exactly, but it was a dark color."

"You know who it could be?" Sylvia said.

"Martha's ex-boyfriend!" Rhonda exclaimed.

"Right. What was his name?"

"Edward...Edward Herman. He's a dairy farmer."

"When did they break up?" I asked.

"About six months ago," Rhonda said. "We saw him only once the entire time we started holding knitting group meetings at the inn. After their breakup, Martha became more and more bitter."

"I don't think their breakup was very civil," Sylvia. "But with Martha, she made a big drama about everything. She was angry a lot."

"Did she ever mention why they broke up?" I asked.

"No," said Rhonda. "Martha never spoke about her personal life. She was hoping to get remarried, and she would rant about how all men were scum anytime one of the knitting group members would start talking about their husbands or boyfriends."

"So you don't know much else about him?" I asked.

Rhonda shook her head. "No. He doesn't live in Hartfield. At least I'd never seen him in town."

"So he lives on a farm, huh?" I said.

"He's a dairy farmer. Not sure where he lives."

Sylvia's eyes were as big as saucers. "Do you think he's the killer?"

Rhonda went pale. "To think that we met a killer!"

"Is Sterling on the case?" Sylvia asked me.

"Yes," I said. "I'll be sure to tell him to look more into Edward Herman."

I paid for the Gouda and thanked the ladies. I was relieved that Rhonda didn't have anything to do with it. Unless of course she was a very good actress sending me on a wild goose chase.

After I left, I immediately called Sterling.

Chapter 6

"We need to talk," I said when Sterling answered his phone.

"About?" He sounded nonchalant, but I knew it was only because he was still hurt.

"I have news about the case. A new lead."

"Okay." He sounded surprised, but he shouldn't have been. He knew how much passion I had for solving mysteries. "Shoot."

"Can I meet you?"

"Well, I'm finishing up my lunch at the office."

"Can I come by?" I asked.

"Does it even matter what I say?" Sterling sighed. "I know you're going to come whether I say yes or not."

I grinned and started heading over to the police station. One of the reasons why I loved Sterling was that he got me, completely. And I got him. Beneath that hard shell, he was a sensitive and intuitive guy who could empathize with people. Which was why

I felt guilty for hurting him. But romance wasn't on my mind right now.

Sterling had his arms crossed when I entered the office. A frosty reception, but I tried to focus on the matter at hand.

"What did you find out?" he asked.

I told him that I had just spoken to Rhonda and Sylvia, and about Edward Herman.

"He's on top of my suspect list too," Sterling said. "Martha's son mentioned that this Edward Herman got into many arguments with Martha when they were together. Once he even laid his hands on her."

"Oh, really?"

"Slapped her right across the face."

"What else did her son say about this guy? Does he know much else about him?"

"Edward wasn't very personable. He doesn't have children of his own, and didn't make much of an effort in getting to know her son. Cal, Martha's son, said they were together for about six months, but they had frequent screaming matches. "

I pulled up a chair and sat across from his desk. "What did they argue about?"

"Martha used to get jealous a lot and often accused Edward of cheating on her."

"Was he?" I asked.

Sterling shrugged. "Cal seems to think so, but he didn't have proof. He didn't stick around to hear them fight."

"Doesn't sound like this Edward stuck around long for the fights either," I said.

"Funny enough, before you came in, I was doing a background check on this guy. He lives alone on his dairy farm thirty minutes from here. He does have a few employees, but they don't live on site. I was just going to go visit him."

"And you're taking me with you, right?"

He shook his head. "I don't think so, Emma."

"Please," I said. "If he's a lady's man as much as Martha claims he is, maybe it wouldn't hurt to have a female with you."

"I thought I was the detective," he said. "I've been doing fine on my own."

"Wasn't I a help on the last case?" I asked.

"Sure, but, that was directly related to you. You don't know who Edward Herman is. He could be dangerous."

"Oh, don't worry. I know Krav Maga. I can defend myself."

Sterling looked at me with amusement. His arms were not crossed anymore and there was a small smile on his face.

"What am I going to do with you?"

"You can take me along to help."

"Fine." He gave an exaggerated sigh and stood up.

"Great!" I put my mittens on. "Let's go."

As we walked out of the station, Sterling got a call.

"Sterling Matthews."

Sterling listened for a bit and then said, "So nothing huh? Keep trying."

He shut off his phone and sighed.

"Forensic hasn't found anything useful so far. No fingerprints, no footprints. It seems like someone had taken care to clean the place — and any evidence along with it. Even the floor is clean and properly washed."

"What? Whoever was there tried to clean around the body?"

Sterling nodded and unlocked the door of his car. "Yup. The killer made an effort to clean up the evidence, or at least the floor, the door handles, things like that. The killer must've cleaned whatever he or she touched, which doesn't seem to be much at this point."

I got in the car and Sterling started the engine. He turned and looked me in the eye.

"Are you sure Nick didn't have anything to do with this?"

"No way he could've done it." I shook my head. "Nick is definitely not a killer."

"Seems a bit odd that he'd sleep through the whole murdering and cleaning up process."

"That's Nick. When he's asleep, he's asleep."

Nick could be oblivious to his surroundings. I guess you could say he was a little self-involved sometimes. Narcissism was expected of a movie star, I supposed, but I didn't excuse him because of that. It drove me crazy.

"So are you guys back together now?" Sterling asked

"No," I said. "Of course not."

I didn't want to have this conversation, but I guessed we had to. We were on the road together for the next half hour. And I did owe Sterling an explanation.

"He came to town with a ring, saying that he wanted to propose. It's what you wanted, right?"

I bit my lip.

"It was," I said slowly. "But that was before I saw you again and..."

"So I made things complicated."

"No! I'm just confused because Nick and I broke up not too long ago, and you and I are pretty new. It's my fault. I mean, I should have taken things slow with us, not that I don't want to be with you, because I do..."

Sterling didn't respond for a while. He kept looking straight ahead. Soon, we were out of Hartfield and surrounded by snowy fields.

"It's not your fault," he finally said. "I have to admit that it was upsetting to me at first. The old Sterling probably would've shut you out, but I want to change. Hell, the way I communicate was one of the reasons I got divorced. So I want to be open with you; I want to let you know that I understand."

"You do?"

He nodded. "It's hard. I'm sure you had very strong feelings for him and it doesn't just shut off like that. But I also know that you feel strongly for me. So I'm not taking myself out of the race. If he's willing to fight for you, I'm going to fight harder."

"Sterling..." I looked at him, but he kept looking at the road. His eyes looked sad, but his expression was full of determination.

"I appreciate it," I said.

"I figured that if you were really set on marrying the guy, you'd decide right away and tell me, right?"

"I would," I admitted.

"So is there anything you want to tell me?"

"No. I'm not together with Nick. However, since he has to stay in town until the investigation ends, he is staying at my house—in a separate room, of course."

A dark cloud passed over his eyes, but he shook it away. "You haven't said yes to him, which means that the chances are still in my favor."

I'd never had two guys compete for me before. It was nice enough to be pursued by one guy that you love, but two?

However, when you loved two guys, it made you doubt the love you had for each of them, which was why I needed more time.

Did I want to live an international, jetsetting, but chaotic lifestyle with Nick, or did I want to settle down in my hometown with my first love? Each of them captured a different side of me and I wasn't sure which side I was in favor of yet.

We didn't talk about it again during the rest of the car ride. Instead, we prepared the questions we'd ask. Sterling would play the bad cop, while I would be the good cop and flirt if necessary. I let my red hair down and applied red lipstick. A bit of mascara made my green eyes pop.

When we reached the farm, we were ready.

Chapter 7

S terling pulled up in front of little gray house at the farm. We rang the doorbell, but nobody answered. We peeked into the windows and saw no one. It was so quiet.

"He must be working in the farm," I said.

We trekked across the snow-covered field to the big red barn. The two doors were closed, and we knocked and waited.

No one answered and we knocked again.

"Anyone there?" I called. "Mr. Herman?"

When there was still no response, I pulled the door open.

The smell of cow manure hit us with full force and we plugged our noses.

"Pee-yew," Sterling said.

"Nothing's more revolting than this," I said.

Inside, dozens of cows formed two long rows. They were hooked up to tubes and contraptions that mechanically milked them. The cows looked miserable and who could blame them? I would be if I were caged and pumped full of hormones so I could lactate for another species' benefit. And to be trapped in a place where you were forced to smell your own stink all day? No thank you.

A man was at the end of the barn. He was far enough away to be only a dark figure. His features emerged the closer he walked to us.

"Are you Edward Herman?" asked Sterling.

"Who's asking?" he said in a cross voice.

The man wore a puffy black down coat over corduroy overalls. He was around sixty, but still lean and tall. Wrinkles lined his dry, chapped skin, but you could tell he used to be a handsome man by his strong bone structure and bright hazel eyes.

"I'm detective Sterling Matthews and this is my partner, Emma. Are you Edward Herman?"

When Edward Herman saw me, he gave me an appreciative smile and a quick once-over.

"Yes," he said. "Sure stinks in here, huh? But don't worry. You'll get used to the smell in a minute. Then you won't smell anything."

"I only pray," Sterling said dryly.

"So what can I do you for?" Edward asked us.

"We're here to ask you a few questions."

Edward took a second look at me. "You look familiar. Have we met?"

I smiled and shook my head. "I don't think so."

"I'm sure I've seen you before." He paused. "Are you on TV?"

How strange that Edward Herman, the dairy farmer, would recognize me out of everyone in town. I could usually run my errands in town without attracting a second look.

"Actually, I'm a singer."

"Emma...Emma Wild?" Recognition struck his face. "Oh, I know you. I mean, I know someone who's a big fan of yours."

"Really?" I said.

"I'd love to get an autograph."

Sterling cleared his throat. This wasn't the time for a fan meeting. He told him we were here about Martha's murder. Edward's face fell.

"Good grief!" Edward exclaimed. "A knitting needle?"

"When was the last time you saw Martha Owens?" Sterling asked.

"We'd broken up months ago. I think Martha drove down to visit me to return a sweater of mine. That was about a month ago."

Sterling raised an eyebrow. "She drove all the way down here just to give you a sweater?"

"Well, I think it was just an excuse. I think she wanted to see me, not that she'd ever admit it. But actions speak louder than words, and I had a feeling she wanted to get back together."

"But you didn't want to?" I asked.

Edward leaned against the rail over one of his cows. He stroked the cow's head.

"No, that relationship was not...ideal."

"Now, what were all the screaming fights between you two about?" Sterling said.

Edward was taken aback by the question. He looked at Sterling and narrowed his eyes, but he answered the question anyway.

"We did used to fight, which was why we broke up. Martha was a bit paranoid and had trust issues. It was because her husband used to cheat on her."

"So you never cheated on Martha?"

Edward balked. "What's this about? Am I a suspect?"

"I'm sorry," I said. "My partner's just doing his job by questioning anyone in connection with her. Anything you know would help us with the case."

Edward regarded Sterling again, but when he looked at me, he softened. "No, I never cheated on Martha. I liked her a lot. I always liked strong women. But all the accusations were getting to me. I couldn't live with her, so I ended it."

"Do you happen to drive a pickup truck?" Sterling asked. "You must since you live on a farm."

"Yes. It's behind the barn. Why?"

"Someone spotted your truck parked in front of Martha's inn on New Year's Eve."

"Why that's impossible -" Edward stopped himself from saying anything else.

"What?" Sterling said. "Where were you that night?"

"I was here," Edward said. "I mean, in my house."

"Alone?" asked Sterling.

Edward opened his mouth but did not answer.

"Was there someone here with you on New Year's Eve?" Sterling repeated with impatience.

"If you have a witness, that would clear you," I said.

Edward relented and nodded. "Yes, there was someone here. But I'm not at liberty to say who."

"Why not?"

"Because." Edward gritted his teeth. "She's married."

We were silent for a moment.

Sterling wasn't rattled. He pressed on.

"So you never cheated on Martha, but you have the morals to get involved with a married woman, huh?"

Edward sighed. "They're not in love. They're only together for the children."

"Who is it?" Sterling asked.

Edward closed his eyes and shook his head.

"I assure you that we're not here to get involved in your personal life," I said. "If you tell us who she is, we will just get her statement privately."

"You promise not to tell her husband?" Edward said.

"As long as you're innocent," Sterling said, "there's no reason to expose your relationship."

Edward breathed hard and rubbed his temples. "All right. If you must know. She's the mayor's wife."

I suppressed a gasp. Mayor Richard Champ's wife, Eleanor, the perfect Stepford wife?

"She has three children," Edward said, "so it's imperative that no one else knows about this. She'll kill me when she finds out that I told you. Richard and Eleanor haven't been in love for years, and he was away for the holidays. Richard doesn't know, so let's just keep it that way. But heck, I wouldn't be surprised if he was cheating himself. They're only together because of his public image as a family man."

He trailed off, looking embarrassed.

"Did Mrs. Champ stay the night?" Sterling asked.

Edward nodded. "Yes."

"We'll speak to her shortly to confirm," Sterling said.

"Can you tell us anything else you know about Martha?" I asked. "Did she have any enemies? Was there anyone else she had disagreements with?"

"Well, it was hard for most people to get along with Martha. She often complained about the women who used to come over and knit. She also complained a lot about her son and they fought often."

"Did they?" I was intrigued. "What about?"

"Martha was quite bossy with him. Telling him what to do all the time and treating him like a baby. Even I was tired of it. There was always something that she wanted him to do, so he never felt good enough. I sympathized with the guy. No wonder he moved out, but it took him long enough. He was living with her until he was thirty! But now I hear he's found a girlfriend and Martha hates her. She was calling her all sorts of names when I last saw her. She always expected Cal to take over running the inn, but he refused. Works as a mechanic now. Good riddance. Otherwise he'd end up a Norman Bates."

"Did they ever get violent with each other?" I asked.

"Not as far as I know," Edward said. "But I wouldn't be surprised if he just snapped one day."

Chapter 8

B y the time we drove back into Hartfield, the sun had already set behind us. Sterling got a last minute call. His partner was asking for help on a separate drug case so we decided to part ways until tomorrow.

When Sterling dropped me off in front of the house, he walked me to the door despite my protests.

"Were you disappointed that it wasn't the dairy farmer?" Sterling asked.

"I thought it could be," I said.

"At least we're another step closer. Another one off my list."

"I just want this case shut already."

"It must mean that you're eager to get Nick out of the house," Sterling said. "Once we catch the murderer, he's free to go. Then I'll have you to myself."

Sterling came closer, wanting to kiss me. I did want to kiss him – his scent was intoxicating–but given that Nick was inside, it didn't seem like a respectful thing to do. I quickly pecked him on the cheek.

"I'll see you tomorrow," I said. Before I could push open the door, I paused and turned around. "Do you really think it could be matricide?"

"I've seen some weird stuff in my career," Sterling said. "I wouldn't be surprised."

"Get some rest," I said.

"Sure. I'll call this mayor's wife in the morning. Come by around ten."

"Sure."

When I entered the house, Nick was walking down the stairs.

"How was your day?" he asked. By the look on his face, I could tell that he had seen Sterling walking me to the door from the top window.

"Fine." I felt guilty, like I was going behind his back.

But I reminded myself that I didn't owe Nick, or Sterling for that matter, anything. I was the one doing Nick a favor by letting him stay at my parents' place while the investigation was under way.

I told him what had happened at the dairy farm and what Edward had said about Martha's son.

"So you think Cal might be the killer?" he said.

"I don't know. But he did seem highly emotional when he saw her body. Maybe it was an act."

"I met Cal once," Nick said. "He joined us for dinner on Christmas Eve. I had just gotten into town and was starving, so when Martha offered some food, I figured I'd eat with them before I set off to see you that evening. Cal was there, but he didn't know who I was. I just said that I was visiting from the states and here to see some friends later that evening."

"How did they behave toward each other?" I asked.

"Martha babied him. Told him to eat this and that, and he groaned when she did that. She even put food on his plate when she thought he wasn't eating enough of a certain dish. He was embarrassed about that, but not angry. We chatted a bit about soccer. He seemed pleasant enough. But he did get agitated a few times throughout the course of the meal when Martha put him down."

"What kind of things would she say?" I asked.

"She'd criticize his hair, his clothes, and his posture, things like that. She'd compare him to me, telling him he should cut his hair like mine, or dress like me. I didn't think it was out of the ordinary. Isn't that what most moms do?"

"And that's why you got along with Martha," I said. "The difference is, she probably doted on you."

Nick had a way with women. His mom also spoiled him a bit too and babied him. Unlike Martha, however, his mom never put him down. Instead, she thought nothing and no one was good enough for him, which meant she didn't approve of me. I was the one she put down. She was too polite to do this outright, but I could tell by the way she looked at my outfit or asked me about my education, which was strange because Nick never went to college either. Nick always said I shouldn't take it personally because she never approved of any girl he dated, but still.

"She kept hinting that he should be working at the inn again," Nick said, "But he'd just groan and change the subject."

"What else do you know about him?" I asked.

"He works as a mechanic. Martha kept badgering for him to quit his job and work at the inn, saying how if he did, business wouldn't be down. She sure did lay a lot of guilt on him. He ate fairly fast and seemed like he was in a hurry to get out of there."

"So eating dinner with her was just a duty to him," I said.

Nick nodded. "Probably. If I was being treated that way, I'd be fed up as well."

"Fortunately, everyone worships the ground you walk on," I teased.

"Well, not everyone." He walked closer and put his hands around my waist.

He pulled me in closer until his nose touched my cheek. Nick smelled amazing too. While Sterling smelled like the ocean, Nick smelled woody, like the forest.

"Dinner's ready," Dad called. He walked out from the living room and saw us. I jumped away from Nick.

"Oh, I'm sorry. Didn't mean to interrupt."

Dad turned and walked right back into the kitchen.

"That was awkward," I said to Nick.

He wasn't as fazed. Nick was always cool, never letting anything ruffle him. He was never at a lack for confidence, a trait I'd always admired.

"Listen, Emma. Why don't I help you?"

"Help me set the table?"

"With the case. I know I'm not a detective, but I am an actor. We study character and we are more conscious of human behavior than psychologists because we embody different personalities. Knowing the motives of a character is the key to acting. Plus, I already know Cal Owens. I can talk to him for you."

"Oh, that's nice of you, but —"

I did promise Sterling that we'd work together. He wouldn't be so happy to have another amateur sleuth tagging along with him, especially not my ex-boyfriend.

"Come on, Emma. I'm cooped up all day reading bad movie scripts. Let me help you. I can go talk to Cal and draw him out for you."

I raised my eyebrows at Nick. I wasn't sure how well he could read people. Sometimes I felt like he took people at face value. He liked everyone, probably because he was used to people liking him. He certainly hadn't been able to read me and my discontent during the relationship for the last few months of our relationship.

But he was a talented actor. His ability to embody characters was more than impressive. Maybe he did have the ability to figure out a person's motives. It was his job.

Maybe he had more in common with Sterling than I realized.

"What would you say to him?" I asked.

"You know me. I can make friends with anyone. I'll ask him to have a beer, talk about his mom, and see what he says."

I considered this. Nick certainly had a charm that could make most people open up. Even Martha liked him. It wouldn't hurt to give it a try.

"All right," I said.

Nick hugged me and kissed me on the top of my head since I was so short.

I was nervous. Sterling wasn't going to like this.

Chapter 9

I n the morning, Nick and I set off for Sterling's office at the police station. Although the walk was only ten minutes, it was so cold because of a nasty snowstorm that we both couldn't take the sharp wind cutting our skin. We were lucky enough to hail a cab and we jumped in and huddled each other for warmth.

"We're supposed to get six inches of snow by tonight." Nick sighed. "I wish we could go skiing."

We went skiing every year, just the two of us. We'd ski in different resorts around the world – Switzerland, British Columbia, France. If we were still together, we would've gone to Aspen this month. Nick was practically a pro, while I was still trying to make it down the bunny slopes on a snowboard without falling on my rump.

"I feel bad that you're stuck in this town," I said. "And, you know, suspected of murder."

Nick groaned. "Say it loud enough for everyone to hear."

Then he leaned forward to address the cab driver with a smile. "I'm not a murderer."

"I sure hope not," the cabbie said.

"Sure I could be living it up somewhere," Nick whispered to me, "but I want to be with you. If that means being suspected of murder, so be it."

He had his arm around me, even though the heat of the cab had long warmed us up.

"You know, Nick. Have you ever considered that you might only want to marry me because of the chase? I know that men enjoy the chase, but once they get what they want, they get bored. How would I know that you really mean it?"

Nick frowned. "Emma, have I ever flaked on you before?"

I thought about it. "No."

"So why don't you trust me?"

Nick had never lied or cheated, but the truth was I expected him to because he had beautiful women surrounding him all the time.

"Because you're...Nick Doyle," I finally said.

"And you're Emma Wild. It took losing you to realize what I had, and I'd be stupid to risk losing you again."

"But I want to have children someday," I said. "Maybe not immediately but within the next five years. If I do, I want to take some time off from music. You're so busy with your career. I hardly even see you as your live-in girlfriend, so I don't know, Nick. I'm not sure if you're ready for such a big commitment. And I also don't want to hold you back from your career."

Nick shook his head. "Emma, you're so stubborn. What do I have to do to show you that I'm willing to do what it takes? I don't have to work back to back. I don't need to prove myself anymore. Maybe when we first started going out, I wasn't ready for marriage, but I'm in my thirties now. I do want to have kids someday too. When you left I realized what a big hole you left. I'm ready now."

I was silent for a moment. I thought about the family life we'd lead, about how much more the paparazzi would hound us.

"We'll figure it out together," said Nick. "Who knows, maybe in a few years, my popularity will take a dive. Nobody might care. Would you still love me then?"

The cab pulled up at the station. I didn't know what to say to Nick. Maybe he did mean it, but he also had a way with words. Sterling, on the other hand, was solid. He always meant what he said. The problem with him was getting him to say it.

We went in and I knocked on Sterling's door. He was happy to see me, but his face fell when he saw Nick.

"What's he doing here?" Sterling asked.

"He wanted to help."

"How?" Sterling said. "He's a murder suspect."

"Am I really still a suspect?" Nick said.

"Yes," Sterling said.

"He's spoken to Cal before," I explained to Sterling. "So Cal knows him already. It might be a good idea for him to take him out to lunch and have a long chat."

"I wouldn't be talking to him as a detective," Nick added. "I'd be talking to him as a friend. Plus, I have a way of getting people to reveal information."

Nick smiled in his self-assured way that some people thought charming and others thought egotistical. Sterling was in the latter category. He scowled.

"I'm not sure you're up for this type of field work," Sterling said.

"Come on," said Nick. "I've jumped off seven story buildings. Danger's my middle name."

"Is it?" Sterling asked dryly.

"No. It's actually Emmett."

Sterling sighed, unamused.

"I had a chat with the mayor's wife," he said. "It's true. They're having an affair. Edward Herman's off the hook."

"Okay," I said. "So what do we know about Cal Owens?"

"I checked and he doesn't own a pickup truck. He owns a silver Honda civic. That said, he does have a record for beating a guy to a pulp in a bar fight when he was in college. He had to pay $5000 and do community service to avoid jail time."

"So he does have a history of aggression," I stated.

"That's a surprise," said Nick. "He didn't seem the type to get into fights. In fact, I thought he was a complete pushover."

"It's always the quiet ones," said Sterling.

"So should we all go pay this guy a visit at the car shop?" I said.

"I want to talk to Cal alone first," said Nick.

Sterling opened his mouth to protest, but I cut in.

"If it doesn't work, you can always interrogate Cal after," I said.

"I'm not an Oscar nominated actor for nothing," said Nick. "Plus, I'm very good at improv and adapting to different situations."

Sterling let out a big sigh. "Fine. But I'm giving you the questions to ask. This guy is our closest lead. He may not own a pickup truck, but he works in a car shop—maybe he has access to one. Are you even sure you can get him to go to lunch?"

"Trust me," said Nick. "He won't be able to say no."

"I guess your charm works on guys and girls," Sterling said.

"It's a power I only use for good," said Nick.

Sterling shook his head. "Let's just get this over with."

Chapter 10

We drove Nick around the corner from Cal's car shop and dropped him off. After we watched him walk in, we parked on the street and waited at the restaurant nearby. If all went to plan, Nick would have lunch in here with Cal soon. We picked a booth where Sterling had his back to the other tables so that Cal wouldn't recognize him.

In the meantime, we ordered lunch. Sterling ordered a cheeseburger while I resorted to a Caesar salad. Lately, I'd been packing on the pounds. Living at home meant eating all of Dad's finest dishes and desserts. Nearly every morning I ate his famous oatmeal cookie pancakes. I had been snacking on his homemade brownie S'mores like crazy that week. The man could start his own comfort food restaurant. I wouldn't mind all the weight gain if it didn't all go to my stomach. My job required that I wore these slinky dresses so I had to start eating healthy and exercising again.

It did make me sad to think that I couldn't stay in Hartfield much longer. My manager, Rod, would soon get over his weeklong hangover and call me at a moment's notice to tell me about some booking for a magazine interview or talk show appearance or other to promote my third album. It was going to be released soon and I had to do the rounds later in the month.

While my first music video was in the can, I had to shoot the video for my second single, but I didn't know where that would take place yet. It was all tiring but fun. For some, it was a fantasy life, but for me it was getting back to reality. Fantasy was staying in my hometown and settling down with family. As much as I loved travelling, I was a homebody at heart.

As if he could read my thoughts, Sterling asked, "So how long are you planning on staying in Hartfield?"

"I know I can't stay in my parents' house forever," I said. "Maybe I'll move back to New York."

"Oh." Sterling looked disappointed.

"For work," I said quickly. "I'm based there for work. It's not too far from Hartfield."

Sterling played with the handle of his coffee mug. "You didn't exactly visit often before."

"I know. But that was because I was scared of running into you all those years."

He gazed into my eyes with tenderness. Thick lashes framed those stormy gray eyes.

"Well you don't need to be anymore." He looked down at his coffee.

Last month, I was single and feeling as if I had failed at love. Now I had two strong prospects to choose from and I didn't want to mess it up. Could I really see myself settling in Hartfield with Sterling? Making him coffee in the mornings as he went off to work and helping him with cases on the side while I composed songs at home? I could. Being a stepmom to his little girls sounded nice as well. I could see myself taking a hiatus as I raised children for a while. Now that I was heading into my thirties, my priorities were changing.

But I also knew I couldn't stop myself from working for long. I loved singing and making music too much to give it up completely. In an ideal world, I would be able to do both. It would probably be difficult for Sterling to get too much time off. If I kept up my career, there would be months when I wouldn't be able to see him because I'd be touring.

"I'll support you in whatever you do," said Sterling. "If that means traveling to New York on the weekends or taking time off to follow you halfway around the world to visit you, I'll do it. I'll always give you the freedom to do what you want."

I smiled. Sterling was the type to sacrifice anything for the people he loved. I squeezed his hand on the table in appreciation.

"I know you would," I said.

He knew how much of a worrywart I was, but he didn't press on the issue any further. I didn't want to think about it either and I was glad when our food arrived so I could perform an action to dig myself out of my slew of nagging thoughts.

Just then, Nick entered with Cal. Cal looked deflated and lifeless, and Nick was trying to cheer him up.

"Don't look back," I whispered to Sterling before I took a bite of my salad.

Cal slid into the booth next to ours and sat with his back to Sterling. Nick spoke loud enough for us to hear.

"Lunch is on me," Nick was saying.

"That's nice of you," said Cal.

"It's the least I could do," said Nick. "I'm just sorry about your loss. Your mom was really gracious and hospitable when I was staying at her inn. How are you doing, anyway?"

Cal sat with his shoulders hunched. He spoke in a listless voice. "I'm okay, considering."

"She treated me like a son," Nick said. "She was nice, wasn't she? Nicer than people think."

Cal nodded slowly. "People do find her unbearable, but she's misunderstood."

He began to cry. I couldn't tell at first, but his whimpers got louder. Nick handed him a tissue, then clapped him on the shoulder.

"Let it out, buddy."

Cal blew his nose out loud. The waitress and the folks at the counter turned to look at him.

"I miss her," Cal said.

"I know." Nick nodded sympathetically. "Do you need help with anything? Are the funeral arrangements taken care of?"

"My dad and his family are flying in from Vancouver tomorrow. They're going to take care of it."

"You don't have any other relatives in this town?"

Cal shook his head. "No. Mom was an only child, and both my grandparents have passed."

"Wow," said Nick. "I guess she was pretty lonely when you moved out, huh?"

"She didn't take it well," said Cal. "She doesn't have too many friends."

"What about all those knitting group ladies?"

Cal blew his nose again. He had stopped crying.

"No. Mom used to complain about how they were all using her for her space. She didn't like them, but

Mom didn't like anyone. I think she only kept them around because their company was better than no company."

"Why did you move out?"

"I was getting too old to live with her," said Cal. "I needed my own life."

"Did you feel guilty at all?"

"Of course, but Mom always made me feel guilty about everything so I got used to it. It didn't affect me the way it would to others."

"What are you going to do about the inn?"

Cal shrugged. "I don't know what we'll do with it yet. We'll probably sell it."

"So you don't want to live at the inn, then?"

"No. My fiancée would never allow it."

"I didn't know you were engaged," said Nick.

"Oh, just recently."

"Congratulations."

"Thanks."

"Did your mom know about your engagement?"

There was a slight pause. "No. She didn't approve of Jasmina. My fiancée is, well, Muslim. My mom was not so...evolved, so she ignored her completely."

"I see," Nick said. "Is that why your fiancée doesn't want to live at the inn?"

"No," said Cal. "Well, she thinks that the inn is spooky. You know, haunted."

Nick chuckled. "I keep hearing that. What do you think?"

"Well, I don't know. Sometimes I do think there are some dark spirits festering in that house. I know that my great grandfather shot himself in the attic."

"Wow."

"And once I was going through the records of the inn and found out that two children had died there in the early 1900s." Cal paused. "It sounds crazy, but sometimes I did think that I could hear children giggling in the corridors."

Nick shuddered. "But you never saw them, did you?"

"Nope," said Cal. "And I never want to. I do wonder if the dark spirits had anything to do with mother's death."

Nick leaned in. "You mean, you think that a *ghost* killed your mother?"

They were interrupted by the waitress, who came by with their drinks and burgers.

"I don't know," said Cal. "But it makes sense, doesn't it?"

"Er, I'm not sure..."

"I know it does sound a little crazy, but there's no other way to explain it."

"When was the last time you saw her?" Nick asked.

"The last time I saw you. For dinner on Christmas Eve. I wanted to visit her on New Year's Eve too, but I had already spent Christmas dinner without Jasmina and left her at home. I wasn't going to abandon her on New Year's too."

Cal sounded defensive. Maybe he was guilty for being a bad son, unless he was guilty for other reasons.

"So you spent New Year's Eve with your fiancée?"

"Yeah. We just sat at home and watched TV. Had dinner, you know." Cal lowered his voice. "So, on that night, you really didn't hear anything? See anything suspicious?"

Nick shook his head before biting into his bacon burger. "I was out like a light. Wish I did though. I did hear from someone else that a pickup truck was spotted outside of the inn."

"What?" Cal exclaimed. "Do the police know?"

"Of course they do." Nick looked at him closely. "Any idea who it could be?"

"A pickup truck?" Cal did some biting and munching of his own. "Why, no. Oh, it could be Edward Herman. He must have a pickup truck."

"No, it wasn't him," said Nick. "He had an alibi."

"Oh." More silence and chewing. "Then I don't know."

I saw Nick looking at him intensely. He said nothing more. For a while, they ate their lunch and we finished ours and then sat there and waited until they left.

Chapter 11

The three of us met back at the car. The snowstorm had stopped, but it left a thick layer of snow on Sterling's car that took some time for him to scrape off.

"What do you guys think?" Nick asked when he got back into the car.

Sterling started the engine. "Something's definitely weird. Ghosts? That's what he could come up with?"

"But the guy would be a damn good actor if he could just cry on command like that," Nick said.

"Maybe he's just a crazy hysteric," said Sterling.

"He did sound a little defensive when you asked him where he was on New Year's Eve," I said. "Maybe he wasn't faking. Maybe he was crying out of guilt."

"When I first questioned him," said Sterling, "he was also shaking and crying a lot. At the time I thought he was upset about his mother, but now with all this ghost talk, I do question his mental well being."

Sterling was way too logical sometimes. I changed the subject.

"Let's go question the fiancée."

"You and I will go," said Sterling. "If Nick comes, it'll be too distracting."

Nick grinned. "Why? Because I'm an international sex symbol?"

"Please," Sterling sneered. "You're just not needed. I'm dropping you at the Wild house."

"Fine," said Nick. "But if you ask me, it's not Cal."

"And how would you know that?" said Sterling.

"It's a little thing called instinct."

Sterling snorted. "We'll see."

"Let's make a bet," said Nick. "If I'm right, Emma belongs with me."

My mouth hung open. "Nick! Don't drag me into this. I'm not something that you can just bet on."

"I agree," said Sterling. "Have some respect, Nick. Besides, Cal is definitely involved. I don't even have to look at his face to know that guilt is written all over it."

"And how would you know that?" Nick asked.

"It's a little thing called years of experience."

After we dropped Nick off, Sterling and I went straight to the apartment building where Cal lived with his girlfriend. The concierge let us in after Sterling showed him his badge. Fortunately, Jasmina was home when we knocked.

"Yes?" She poked her head out the crack of the door.

She was pretty, with dark eyes lined with black eyeliner, dewy dark skin and shiny long black hair. No wonder Cal would rather live with her than with his mother.

"I'm detective Sterling and this is my partner, Emma. We're here to ask you some questions about your fiancé."

Jasmina frowned. "Fiancé? How did you know that we were engaged?

"Can we please come in?" I asked.

She stared at me for a second. "Do I know you?"

Then recognition flashed in her eyes. "Oh, you look exactly like Emma Wild, the singer."

"I get that a lot," I said.

"And didn't you say your name is Emma too?'

"A coincidence." I smiled.

She opened the door and let us in.

"I'm sorry about the mess," she said. "I would've cleaned if I knew I would have company."

The apartment was spotless. I didn't know what mess she was referring to. The living room was spacious with huge windows facing a park. She sat down on a beige sofa while Sterling sat on the couch. I remained standing.

"Where were you on New Year's Eve?" Sterling began.

"Here," she said. "In this apartment."

"And where was Cal Owens?"

"Here, with me."

"At any point, did he leave this apartment?" Sterling asked.

"No. We were here the entire evening. We ate dinner, watched the countdown, then went to sleep. What's this about?"

"Have you ever visited his mother, Martha Owens?"

Jasmina's face twitched, or was I just imagining things?

"I did see her about a month ago, but not since."

"And what did you think of her?"

Jasmina paused. "Is this about her murder?"

Sterling nodded.

"Well, she wasn't exactly happy to see me. She didn't approve of me, because of my...race. I didn't stay long."

"And you hadn't seen her since?" I asked.

She shook her head.

"What was Cal's relationship like with his mother?" asked Sterling.

"Are you here because you suspect Cal of killing his own mother?"

"We'll be asking the questions," said Sterling.

Jasmine looked agitated and shot him a dirty look, but she answered anyway.

"His mother was a little overbearing, but Cal would never hurt her. He would never hurt a fly."

"The same Cal Owens who broke a man's nose in a bar fight?"

"That was ages ago," said Jasmina.

"So you knew about that?"

"Yes. He was in college, and drunk. He was young back then. It doesn't mean that he's a murderer. Like I said, Cal was with me all night. He loves his mother. He would never do anything like that."

I paced in the living room behind the couch Sterling was sitting on, observing the apartment. I looked out the window, down into the parking lot. A vehicle stuck out to me, but I didn't want to interrupt yet. There was something else that intrigued me as well.

"Are you a knitter?" I asked Jasmina.

She had a knitting bag beside the sofa. It looked like she was starting a scarf with cable stitching.

"Yes," Jasmina said. "Is that a crime too?"

I didn't say anything. She sounded defensive, but she had every right to be.

Just then, there were footsteps down the hallway. The door opened and Cal burst in and slammed the door behind him.

"Jasmina!" he said. "They know about the pickup truck. We have to get rid of it."

He was panting because he'd been running and in such a daze that he didn't notice Sterling and me sitting at the side of the living room.

"So you do drive a pickup truck," Sterling said, standing up.

When Cal saw us, his face turned pale. He opened his mouth, but nothing came out.

"It was you, wasn't it?" Sterling said. "You went to visit your mom on New Year's Eve, but a simple visit turned into an argument and you killed your mother in the midst of it. Then you covered it up by wiping your fingerprints from the knitting needle, cleaned the place up and ran."

Cal sat down and began to cry again. I'd never seen a man cry so much in my life.

"It was me," Cal said. "I did it. I killed my mother."

Chapter 12

Nobody said anything for a moment. Cal was crying on the floor and everyone froze, watching him break down.

"It was an accident," said Cal. "We got into an argument. I felt bad about leaving her alone on New Year's Eve, but when I got there, she was angry."

"And you stabbed her?" I asked.

Sterling took out a pair of handcuffs and went over to handcuff Cal, but I stopped him.

"I'm still not convinced it is Cal," I said.

"But he just confessed," said Sterling.

"Yes, but what was Jasmina doing there on New Year's Eve?"

Jasmina looked shocked. Sounds came out of her mouth, but she couldn't speak.

"It was your pickup truck, wasn't it?" I said. "And your scarf that I found in the bottom of Martha's trash can in the kitchen. You went with Cal to Martha's inn, and gave her a present, but Martha didn't want it, did she? She insulted you, and you reached for the needle and struck her in the chest. Then you cleaned away the evidence, didn't you?"

Jasmina began to sob herself. "Yes, it was me. Cal was just trying to cover for me. I killed Martha."

"Jasmina didn't mean to do it!" Cal exclaimed. "We had both been drinking, and she doesn't handle her liquor well. When my mom lunged at her, she was only trying to defend herself."

Jasmina hung her head and buried her face in her palms. We waited until she calmed down and then she spoke.

"Cal and I have been together for two years. Martha had never accepted me. She just wanted to control Cal and keep him chained to her side. I was sick and tired watching her emasculate him. She just saw me as a threat, but I tried to get along with her for Cal's sake. On New Year's Eve we hadn't planned on visiting her, but at the last minute, we felt bad for leaving her alone. Cal's car was in the shop, so we took my truck."

"Why do you have a pickup truck anyway?" asked Sterling.

"It was my dad's," said Jasmina. "He passed away last year and left it to me. I thought that New Year's Eve might be a good time to talk to Martha again, so she would give us the blessing to get married. The new year was a time to put past disagreements behind us. Cal valued her approval and I guess I did too. I brought along a scarf I knitted, because I knew that she appreciated homemade knits. If she didn't want it, she could've at least donated it to the sick children along with the things that she made. But no, Martha had to get nasty about it. She spat on my scarf and threw it in the trash! She called me horrible racist names and attacked me, my family, and my religion. Then she called Cal a traitor, calling him a loser for resorting to being with someone like me..."

Jasmina continued to sob and Cal stumbled over to hug her.

"It was all too much for me to take," she said between the tears. "Martha was getting aggressive, yelling and coming closer and in my tipsy state, I thought she was going to kill me, so I grabbed the closest thing I could find and—"

She sobbed into Cal's chest. Cal stroked her head and whispered, "It's okay, it's okay."

"Why didn't you just come forward?" said Sterling. "You would've had a much lighter sentence."

"We got scared," said Cal. "I didn't want Jasmina in jail. We wanted to get married and start a life together. So I told her that we should clean up and nobody would know."

"But you tried to blame it on the dairy farmer," I said.

"It was stupid," said Cal, "but we were desperate. I never liked that bastard Herman anyway. He laid his hands on my mother."

"But *ghosts*, for Pete's sake," Sterling exclaimed. "You tried to blame your mother's murder on ghosts."

"That house *is* haunted," said Jasmina. "I'll never step foot in it again."

"I'm sure that the evil spirits had something to do with what happened," said Cal.

"All that negativity swirling in there," said Jasmina, shaking her head. "I'm sure that I was possessed somehow, momentarily."

Sterling made a phone call to the police station.

When he hung up, he looked them both in the eyes. "The good news is, at least you can plead for insanity."

Chapter 13

"So I was right," Nick said. "Cal didn't do it. I win."

"Wrong," said Sterling. "Cal wasn't innocent. He tried to help his fiancée cover up her murder. He's just as guilty. Looks like I win."

Sterling had dropped me off at home and Nick came out to get the scoop.

"What did I tell you guys?" I fumed. "I'm not to be bet on and claimed."

"Oh," Sterling said. "Sorry."

"How did you know that the scarf in the trash was Jasmina's?" asked Nick.

"It was the same color and the same stitching as the material on Jasmina's throw on the couch. She was also in the middle of knitting another scarf with the same pattern. Adding in the fact that she loved to clean, I just knew it was her."

"Brilliant," said Nick.

Nick and Sterling both looked at me with such adoration that I blushed.

"I'm just glad this is all over," I said. "It's so sad. They just wanted to get married."

Sterling shook his head. "An unfortunate event. Anger is a dangerous thing, more dangerous than any firearm."

"I hope her sentence is not too harsh," I said. "Poor thing. I'm sure it was hard to have been the recipient of racism, especially coming from your own fiancé's mother."

"Still, that's no excuse for murdering someone," said Nick.

"Yes," I agreed. "It's just an all-round horrible situation."

"You never actually thought I killed Martha, did you?" Nick asked Sterling.

"No," Sterling replied. "I wanted you behind bars, but my instinct ultimately told me no."

"I guess we both have pretty strong instincts."

They turned to me again, looking at me with a mixture of adoration and expectation. I was used to being looked at by thousands in a stadium or millions on TV, but these two men made feel like shrinking into myself.

"It's been a long day," I said. "Thanks for everything, Sterling."

He leaned in and kissed me on the cheek goodnight.

I was glad that he was gracious enough to shake hands with Nick.

"And how long will you remain in town?" Sterling asked.

Nick rubbed the back of his neck. "Well, I got a call from my agent earlier this afternoon. The studio wanted to reshoot some fighting scenes in Morocco, so I'll have to ship out in a couple of days."

"I see," said Sterling.

I didn't say anything. I didn't expect Nick to leave so soon. I was hoping for more time to make a decision.

"You'll miss me, won't you?" Nick teased Sterling, grinning.

"Hmm," Sterling said. "Well, I suppose the question is, will Emma be going with you?"

They turned to me for the third time and I took a deep breath.

"I know it's not fair that I haven't made up my mind, and I'm sure you're eager to know so that you can move on with your lives. If I had to choose right now, I'd pick, well, no one. I want some time alone to figure some stuff out. You know I do have feelings for the both of you, but I'm causing more pain by delaying this decision, so I just want you to be happy. If you can be with another girl who is one hundred percent sure about you, I won't get in the way."

Sterling frowned. "Are you sure that's what you want?"

"It is," I said. "It's been so chaotic this holiday season. I'd just like to spend some time with my family and figure out my next career move, settle down a bit before I make any important life decisions."

"I'm willing to wait for your decision," said Nick. "As long as Sherlock here doesn't try to put the moves on you while I'm away."

Sterling shot him a look. "I'm willing to give Emma the space, just as long as you don't bombard her with calls."

"Fine," said Nick. "It's fair if we both give Emma some space while I'm gone for the month so that she has the clarity to come to her senses and pick me."

Sterling rolled his eyes. "Oh, please."

All things considered, Nick and Sterling were handling this very well. In the movies, when two guys were fighting over a girl, they often got violent. These two actually considered me and my feelings over what they really wanted. This was about to make my decision even harder.

"I appreciate it," I said to both of them. "I think a month will be long enough. By the time Nick finishes his reshoot, I'll let both of you know. In the meanwhile, I won't be in contact with either of you."

"You can count on me," Sterling said, staring Nick down.

"I won't call, I swear." Nick met Sterling's gaze and held it.

"Thanks for being so great about this," I said.

Nick came downstairs with his leather duffel bag, ready to go.

"We'll miss you, dear." Mom gave Nick a hug.

"Can't wait for *Dead and Alive 2*," said Dad. "Opening day, I'll be in that theater."

"Thanks Mr. Wild." Nick grinned.

My parents went into the kitchen to leave us alone. Mom gave me an encouraging smile.

"This is it," said Nick.

"Have fun in Morocco," I said. "Don't break anything, like last time."

Nick had sprained his ankle during an action scene when he shot the film months ago. I had been worried to death. He was lucky he didn't break any bones. For this film, he had to jump from one building to the next, parachute, and fight from day to night. It would be physically draining.

Nick noticed the worry on my face.

"I'll be fine," he said. "I'm like a cat. I always land on my feet."

"Okay," I said dubiously.

"Just know that I'll be thinking of you," he said. "Even if I can't call you, or hear your voice. I'll just watch videos of you online singing."

"No!" I laughed. "Don't. And don't read the YouTube comments. They are so mean."

His cab was here. Nick put on his wool coat and I hugged him. He smelled like someone I'd miss already. I'd missed him before and I knew I'd miss him again.

He held me in the embrace but tilted his head back to look at me.

"But seriously," he said. "I'll be thinking of you. I'll imagine you next to me and talk to you out loud."

"I hope you don't do that in front of the crew."

Before I could stop him, he kissed me on the lips. It was an all consuming, all devouring kiss, the same kind that had left me breathless many times before.

"Now you'll have to think about me too," he said when he pulled away.

"Nick…" I began to scold. But he looked so adorable that I didn't.

I opened the door. I watched him get into the cab. He waved from the back as the cab drove off, just like in the movies. I stood in the middle of the street, waving back, feeling a pang in my heart.

The street was calm, the snow was fresh, and the wind grazed my cheeks. I hugged myself in my oversized knitted sweater as I walked back to the house.

It was the new year.

Time to start anew.

With no boys around me, I could focus on my own life and figure out what was really important.

Despite all the flurry of emotions running through me, I was looking forward to that little piece of freedom.

Recipe 1

Martha's Blueberry Scones

- 4 cups all-purpose flour
- 1 1/2 cups fresh or frozen blue-berries (if frozen, don't thaw to avoid discoloring batter)
- 2 eggs
- 6 tbsp sugar
- 3/4 cup + 2 tbsp milk
- 4 1/2 tsp baking powder
- 1/2 tsp salt
- 1/2 cup + 2 tsp cold butter

Combine flour, sugar, baking powder and salt; cut in butter until mixture resembles coarse crumbs.

In another bowl, whisk eggs and 3/4 cup milk. Add to dry ingredients just until moistened. Turn onto a lightly floured surface and gently knead in the blueberries.

Divide dough in half. Pat each portion into an 8-inch circle. Cut each circle into 8 wedges. Place on greased baking sheets. Brush with milk.

Bake for 15-20 minutes at 375 degrees F or until tops are golden brown. Makes 16 scones.

Recipe 2

Dad's Brownie S'mores

- 1 package brownie mix

- 1 1/2 cups miniature marshmallows

- 6 graham crackers

- 8 bars milk chocolate, coarsely chopped

Preheat oven to 350 degrees F (175 degrees C). Prepare brownie mix according to the box directions and spread into a greased 9x13 pan.

Break the graham cracks into 1-inch pieces into a medium bowl along with the marshmallows and milk chocolate. Set aside.

Bake brownies for 15 minutes. Remove and sprinkle the s'more mixture on top. Bake for an additional 15-20 minutes, or until a toothpick inserted in the center comes out clean. Allow brownies to cool before cutting into squares.

Recipe 3

Dad's Oatmeal Cookie Pancakes

- 1 cup all-purpose flour
- 1 cup old fashioned oats
- 2 large eggs
- 2 really ripe bananas, mashed
- 1/2 cup brown sugar
- 2 tsp baking powder
- 1/2 tsp baking soda
- 1 tsp ground cinnamon
- 1/4 cup (2 ounces) chopped walnuts
- 3/4 cup sour cream
- 3/4 cup whole milk
- 3/4 cup raisins
- 1/2 stick butter + 1/4 cup melted butter

- 1 tsp vanilla extract

- Honey or maple syrup for drizzling

Mix dry ingredients (oats, flour, sugar, baking powder, baking soda, cinnamon, walnuts) in a bowl.

In another bowl, mix the sour cream, whole milk, eggs, and vanilla. Whisk this into the dry ingredients until combined, then fold in mashed bananas and raisins. Stir in melted butter.

Heat pan on medium and brush with melted butter. Cook pancakes (around 1/3 cup each) until bubbles form on top. Then turn. Cakes will cook in 2 minutes on each side. Serve with honey or maple syrup drizzled on top.

To keep pancakes warm, cover with a piece of foil.

About the Author

Harper Lin lives in Kingston, Ontario with her husband, daughter, and Pomeranian puppy. When she's not reading or writing mysteries, she's in yoga class, hiking, or hanging out with her family and friends. She lived in Paris in her twenties, which inspired *The Patisserie Mysteries*.

She is currently working on more cozy mysteries.

www.HarperLin.com

New Year's Slay

Made in the USA
Las Vegas, NV
02 January 2022

40114488R00069